Fancy NANCY

Aspiring Artist

Aspiring means I hope to become a good artist!

Written by Jane O'Connor • Illustrated by Robin Preiss Glasser

HARPER

An Imprint of HarperCollinsPublishers

To Ellie and Jessica, the ever-so-fancy Sassienie Honeyball sisters
—J. O'C.

For my mother, Marcia Preiss, who made me my first art smock
—R.P.G.

La Gerbe by Henri Matisse
© 2010 Succession H. Matisse / Artists Rights Society (ARS), New York
Collection University of California, Los Angeles. Hammer Museum. Gift of Mr. and Mrs. Sidney F. Brody.

One: Number 31 by Jackson Pollock
© 2010 The Pollock-Krasner Foundation / Artists Rights Society (ARS), New York
Jackson Pollock. One (Number 31, 1950).
Oil and enamel on unprimed canvas, 8' 10" X 17' 5 ⅝". Sidney and Harriet Janis Collection Fund (by exchange).
The Museum of Modern Art, New York, NY, U.S.A.
Photo credit : Digital image © The Museum of Modern Art/Licensed by SCALA / Art Resource, NY

Rehearsal of the Ballet on the Stage by Edgar Degas
42-18372063
© The Gallery Collection/Corbis

The Artist's Garden at Giverny by Claude Monet
42-18300183
© The Gallery Collection/Corbis

Fancy Nancy: Aspiring Artist
Text copyright © 2011 by Jane O'Connor
Illustrations copyright © 2010, 2011 by Robin Preiss Glasser
All rights reserved. Manufactured in China.
No part of this book may be used or reproduced in any manner whatsoever without written permission
except in the case of brief quotations embodied in critical articles and reviews. For information address
HarperCollins Children's Books, a division of HarperCollins Publishers,
10 East 53rd Street, New York, NY 10022.
www.harpercollinschildrens.com

Library of Congress Cataloging-in-Publication Data is available.
ISBN 978-0-06-212857-7

Typography by Jeanne L. Hogle
14 15 16   LEO   10 9 8 7 6 5 4 3
❖
First Edition

Sunday

It's spring vacation, so I should be ecstatic, joyous, carefree. (Those are all fancy words for happy.) But I'm not. Bree and her family just left for New York City, the glamour capital of the world.

My mom knows I am a little
glum, which is sad in a fancy way.
So when she comes back from
grocery shopping, she has treats—
a big box of **crayons** for my sister
and a set of glitter **markers** for me.

What a **splendid** parent my mother is!

While I'm doodling with my new markers, inspiration strikes. That means I get a great idea. I will turn my clubhouse into an art studio and spend my vacation making gorgeous works of art.

Doodles don't really count as art, but I get some of my most splendid ideas while doodling.

Besides some supplies—that's fancy for markers, paints, and paper—all you need in an art studio is an artist! I'm wearing a smock and a beret. That's French for cap.

Don't you think my beret makes me look more talented?

My sister can only scribble. Even though scribbling doesn't count as real art, I tell her how beautiful her pictures are.

In the afternoon I have dance class. All over the studio
are posters of ballerinas by a French artist named Edgar Degas.
While I am *plie*-ing, suddenly inspiration strikes!

I return to my art studio and draw beautiful ballerinas, just like Edgar Degas did.

(Do you notice who all the ballerinas look like? Hee hee.)

Monday

Today I tell Mrs. DeVine about my art studio. Her favorite artist is Claude Monet. She tells me he didn't like to work in a studio. He loved painting outdoors, even in winter. He'd wear three coats and a blanket to keep from freezing. Brrr!

Suddenly inspiration strikes again! "I would love to paint outdoors in your garden, just like Claude Monet."

It was sunny when I painted this. I call it *Tulips in the Wind*.

Then some clouds came and I had to use darker colors to paint the same flowers. I call this *More Tulips in the Wind*.

Tuesday

I invite my friend Lionel over today. He can act like a real goofball, but he is the most talented artist in our class. His faces are so good. Nobody does noses like Lionel. (Not to brag, but I am the second most talented—you can ask anybody.)

Here is a portrait Lionel drew of me. A portrait is a picture of someone's face. Hee hee. I don't really have a mustache or a goatee (that's fancy for a short beard).

Then Lionel poses for me, but he keeps making crazy faces.
Lionel is such a goofball!

Here is a joke Lionel told me. What color is a burp?
Burple!

Wednesday

Ooh la la—a letter from Bree! I adore getting mail, don't you?
Look what she did on the back of the envelope. She wrote SWAK.
That means "sealed with a kiss."

Here is the front of the card Bree sent. She went to a world-famous museum where she saw this picture by Henri Matisse. He made it from pieces of colored paper that he cut out.

Inspiration strikes once more!
I get construction paper, glue, and scissors and . . .

Voilà! I make a picture like Henri Matisse did.

Even though wings on real butterflies always match, mine
have two different wings. Artists are allowed to break rules!

Thursday

Even though I have been in the studio for hours, everything I draw today stinks.

My mom comes in to tell me that Lionel's grandma called. "She's taking him to a 3-D movie and he wants you to come."

"Alas, I can't go," I say. "I'm waiting for inspiration to strike."

"Nancy, it's wonderful to be dedicated—that means working really hard," my mom tells me. "But take a break! It will get your creative juices flowing again." (My mother knows I listen better when she uses fancy words.)

Can you buy creative juice?

No! It's a fancy phrase for imagination.

My mom was right. After I get home, my creative juices start flowing. The movie was about really weird fish that live on the bottom of the ocean. Mine are imaginary—that means I made them up.

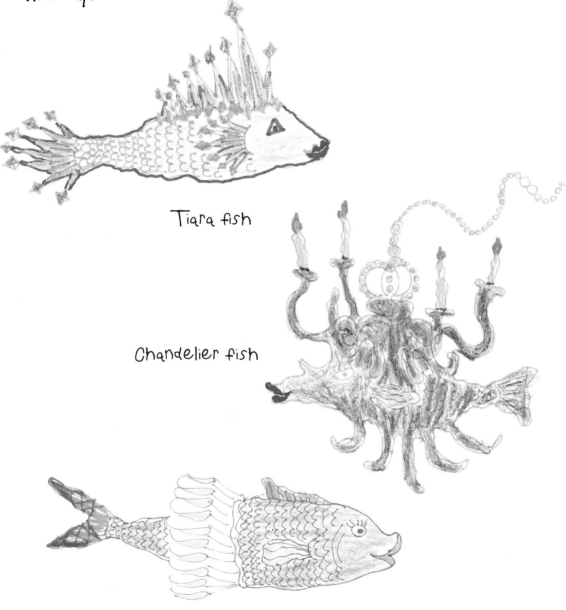

Tiara fish

Chandelier fish

Tutu fish

For a special treat, my dad is taking us to the art museum. Lionel comes too. On the way over, he pretends to be carsick. My dad starts to pull over, but I explain that Lionel is just being a goofball.

At the museum, there is a real painting by Claude Monet. I wish I knew a fancy word for how it makes me feel. All I can say is the colors make my eyes happy, and my heart happy too.

Lionel says he likes this painting. At first I think he's kidding. It's just a big bunch of black drips and blobs. But the harder I look, the more interesting it is. Some parts look lacy. One part is almost like a spiderweb. My dad really likes it too.

My dad tells us he once saw a movie about the artist Jackson Pollock. "He put the canvas on the floor and poured on paint straight from the can. He also used paint sticks to make dribbles and all kinds of patterns."

Inspiration strikes again. I turn to Lionel. "We could make a big painting like Jackson Pollock. We'll do it tomorrow when Bree is back."

Saturday

At last, Bree and I are reunited. (That's fancy for being together again.)

I tell her it's officially Jackson Pollock Day. (Not really, but doesn't it sound important?)

My parents spread out a
sheet in the backyard and find
leftover cans of house paint.

We wear old clothes, put on
hip-hop music for inspiration, and then ... Ooh la la!
We fling and flick paint.
We make swirls and splatters.
We drip and dribble.
We are painting and dancing at the same time.

Jackson Pollock was a very serious professional artist, but making a painting this way is silly and fun!

Later I show Bree all my art from this week. She shows me her sketches from New York City. My mom tells Lionel to stop sticking carrot sticks up his nose. Then she says, "You have so much art, you could have an art show."

What a splendid idea!

We hang all our artwork
on the clothesline.

by: Nancy

JoJo

We make a sign
for the front yard
announcing the exhibit.
Exhibit is a fancy word
for show.

Come See the
work of local
ARTists
Free refreshments
Sunday from 2-3

Atlantic City

Sunday

Our art exhibit is a smashing success. (That's a fancy way to say everyone has a good time and tells us how talented we are.)

I give Mrs. DeVine one of the paintings I did in her garden.
I tell her, "I can't believe how tired my hands are from all the
art I made this week!"

Mrs. DeVine says that she knows the perfect remedy for
aching artist hands . . .

a manicure!